W9-CGY-779

# WAKING
# BEAUTY

OR ELEVEN TIMES UPON A TIME

# REBECCA SOLNIT

•

WITH ILLUSTRATIONS BY
# ARTHUR RACKHAM

Text © 2022 Rebecca Solnit
Illustrations by Arthur Rackham

Published in 2022 by Haymarket Books
P.O. Box 180165, Chicago, IL 60618
www.haymarketbooks.org

ISBN: 978-1-64259-833-9

Haymarket Books offers discounts for organizations
and schools for orders of ten copies or more.

Cover design by Abby Weintraub. Book design
by Abby Weintraub and Rachel Cohen.
Typeset in 14pt Hoefler Text.

Illustrations based on Arthur Rackham's paintings
appearing in the 1920 edition of *Sleeping Beauty*,
published by William Heineman, London,
and J. B. Lippincott Co., Philadelphia,
and in *The Fairy Tales of the Brothers Grimm,*
published by Doubleday, Page & Co
in New York in 1909.

Printed in Canada.

1 3 5 7 9 10 8 6 4 2

# IDA,
## or SLEEPING BEAUTY

Once upon a time there was a child named Ida, and wild things happened to her.

❧

But that's not where the story begins. Before there was Ida there was her mother and father, and before them their parents, and before them...

Before every beginning is another beginning. Before there is a child, there are parents. Whether she has one parent in her life or five or is raised by aunts or wolves or elves.

Ida had two human parents, so perhaps this story should begin,

"Twice upon a time...." Or, since two parents and one child make three, "Three times upon a time."

⤳

Her parents had fairy godmothers, seven of them.

So we could also start, "Seven times upon a time."

The first fairy's real name was

Incandescent Lumina Popsicle Jones,

and the second one's name was

Dreamsicle Swantooth Felicidada,

and the other five were even worse.

Everyone called them Monday, Tuesday, Wednesday, Thursday, Friday, Saturday, and Sunday.

They were good fairies, all of them, but Sunday was so good she was awful. Sunday thought everything should be perfect, and she was always showing up to complain that things were not what they were supposed to be. At a picnic, for example, she would complain that the strawberry jam should be blackberry, and then eat all the strawberry jam anyway.

If you told her you liked her hat, she thought that meant you hated her shoes, and her favorite question was always "What's wrong with this?" except when it was "Whose fault is this?" She was the great killer of parties and the spoiler of games. That's a magical power that you should try not to have.

Her full name was

Marzipanzer

Divisadero

Primrooseveltundramama

McIrritabittlepittlegram,

which is why at least there's one thing to be glad about her: that we can call her Sunday.

The story about why she was that way begins a long time ago, when Wednesday's pet griffin ate Sunday's birthday cake when they were very young. For fairies, very young means about a thousand years old. It is true that a thousandth birthday cake is often very large, with a lot of candles, so if a griffin eats it all, it's quite a loss.

Once upon a time, or twice, or more, two parents had their first child and invited a lot of people and seven fairy godmothers to the child's name day.

(Once upon a time

plus twice

plus seven

is ten times upon a time.)

The invitations were written by hand on yellow paper in beautiful inky blue letters and were very nice, and they went into green envelopes

and the envelopes went into the mail.

The mail went into a red bag

and the bag went on the back of a horse that the messenger rides

and the horse galloped by a rosebush

and the rosebush had thorns

and a thorn tore the bag

and one invitation fell out

and the horse didn't notice

and neither did the rider

and the invitation fell into the road

and then rain fell and the ink ran

and a herd of goats walked over it

so it got covered by mud

and was never seen again

except by worms and beetles
and a mouse who spent a rainy afternoon under it
but the mouse's story is another story.

Unfortunately the lost envelope held the name-day invitation to Sunday.

～

The name day came, and so did the guests, and there were fireworks and there was cake and there was a nice speech by Thursday about love and some presents from the six fairies and other presents from the other people. The baby was named Ida, and she didn't cry very much at her party, and they only had to change her diaper once, and lots of people held her and said what a nice smile she had, and wished her well.

And then Sunday came, and that was so terrible we have to start another chapter about how awful it was. And horrible. Ugly. Mean. Wrong. Bad.

⤳

Sunday came in like thunder, and she shouted, *Why didn't you invite me*, and she didn't wait for the answer, which was that they did, or they tried to, so there must be some mistake. Sunday did not believe in mistakes or accidents. While the other fairies were in the middle of giving gifts, Sunday cursed the baby.

She said in a voice like thunder, only more grumpy,

*When Ida is fifteen she will prick her finger on a spindle and die!*

And then she flashed like lightning and vanished into a stormcloud, so that no one could argue with her about what a nasty thing to do that was.

(We will talk about what spindles are later.)

Friday and Saturday hadn't given their gifts yet, and so they worked and strained and called on all their magic power and bent the big curse into a smaller curse. When curses are freshly made and still soft they can be bent or sometimes tied in a knot or even taken back.

*She won't die*, said Saturday, *but she will sleep for a hundred years.*

*I'm sorry*, said Friday, *but that's the best we can do.*

Thursday said, *You never really know what will happen. Maybe something interesting will come of this.*

5

Wednesday said, *I do love sleep.*
Tuesday bounced the baby and burped her.
Monday poured some more tea.

‿ə‿

I forgot to mention that Ida's mother was the song queen of the kingdom
of Zur, and the family lived in the great stone palace on the banks of the
river Amandla.

Ida had a beautiful singing voice and she learned the queen's main job,
which was to sing the song that made the cherry trees bloom.
She also learned other songs about the birds coming back in the spring
and why the rabbits dance in the dew in the grass at dawn
and the one about rainy days
and the one about the boy who turned into a bear
until he found the bear that had turned into a boy,
and they both changed back, and went home to
their families.

She even learned what songs the
mermaids sing,
and sometimes when the moon was new
she would go down to the sea at night
and listen to them sing their mermaid
songs
full of mermaid stories about how compli-
cated life is under the sea.
Sometimes she would sing with
them a little, and voices would fly up
from the rocks and down from the cliff.

6

The Amandla River flows down to the sea, and on the rocks near the shore the mermaids sit and comb their hair and sing, because their hair gets full of seaweed and barnacles, and because why not sing while you work if you can sing like a mermaid?

Once upon another time, longer ago, the Queen of Zur ruled over everyone, but people got tired of being bossed around, so they made all the big decisions together at meetings. (Sometimes the meetings went on forever, because someone talked too much, but it was still better than having one person boss everyone around.). But since Zur on the banks of the Amandla River was a magic country, the queen in that time had magic powers that passed on from mother to oldest daughter. She wasn't the only one with magic powers, but she was the only one with *that* magic power.

By powers we mean responsibilities, and one responsibility was to sing the songs that made the cherry trees flower in the springtime so there would be cherries on the trees in the summer and cherry jam all winter.

She wasn't the only queen either. There was a queen of butterflies and a queen of windmills and a queen of camping and so many other queens.

⤳

Ida's parents asked everyone to burn up all the spindles in the land. People did it because the two parents were very upset and they explained why they needed that done.

A spindle is a tool that people use to spin thread, and unless you spin thread, you can't weave cloth, and if you can't weave cloth you can't make clothes (or mailbags or flags or blankets or tents). A spindle looks like a stick, and sometimes it's sharp at one end. It's called a spindle because you spin it so it twists the stuff you're holding into thread.

They also destroyed the spinning wheels that are another way people make thread. There were big bonfires. They thought they could stop Sunday's curse if they made all the spindles and spinning wheels go away.

In those once-upon-a-time days, people made clothes by hand, starting with the wool from the sheep or the linen from the flax in the fields or the silk from the silkworms on the mulberry trees. Because it was so much work to make clothes, people never threw them out. But with the spindles destroyed, people had to wear clothes that got older and older.

With the spindles destroyed, there was no thread to weave with. So the weavers were out of work, and they stopped making cloth. Then the tailors and seamstresses who sewed the cloth into clothes were out of work too. Though they found a little work cutting up old clothes to make new ones and making wedding dresses out of curtains and winter coats out of blankets.

That was a bad thing, but other things happened too. One of the good ones was the birth of Ida's little sister Maya, and that's when this story becomes Eleven Times Upon a Time.

(Once for Ida,

Twice and three times for her mother and father,

Seven Times for the Seven Fairies,

and One More Time for Maya makes Eleven Times

Upon a Time.)

Maya and Ida were just alike and completely different. Maya couldn't sing at all but she could draw. Both of them liked to dance, but Ida liked to climb trees and Maya liked to swim, and one of them liked strawberries best and the other one liked blackberries best, and sometimes they fought and sometimes they played.

Maya often thought it was much better to be Ida, and Ida often thought it was better to be Maya. And of course they complained about it.

*Why do I have to learn the songs and Maya doesn't have to?*

*Why don't I get to learn the songs that Ida learns?*

*Why can't I draw like Maya?*

*Why can't I sing like Ida?*

And both of them:

*Why does everyone like my sister better?*

*Why is it my turn to clean the kitchen?*

And so forth, about who had curlier hair and who had a better birthday party and whether it was easier to be the younger one or the older one.

But they didn't complain all the time, and sometimes they had fun, like when they turned the drainspouts in on the south tower and all the rainwater poured down the stairs like a waterfall, or when they chased the sheep into the museum or trained the dog to dance or climbed the tree so high they could see the mountains behind the hills.

Then came the day their parents were dreading, the day Ida turned fifteen, the day when girls in Zur had their first dance party. Ida's parents had never told her about Sunday's curse.

Ida woke up before anyone else and thought that maybe there were some trunks of dress-up clothes in one of the towers no one had found yet, so she got up early and ran around and looked and looked in the south tower and the north tower and the east tower and she found some very interesting things.

But she didn't find any dress-up clothes there,
and so she went where Ida and Maya were never supposed to go:
through the tunnel under the old part of the castle
and through the long hall
and the room as big as a barn full of rusty weapons from the old wars gone by,
to the dusty steps to the west tower.
Dusty and full of spiderwebs, but they didn't stop her.

At the top was an old door and it creaked when she pushed it open. The voice of the old woman sitting there sounded just like the door as she creaked, *Happy birthday, Ida!*

Ida was surprised, but she was also interested in what the woman was doing with a cloud of some kind of stuff and a thing kind of like a stick and a twisting movement of her hands. She had never seen it before. *Thank you*, she said, because she was a polite child, and then,

*What are you doing?*

*I am spinning wool into thread, my dear*, said the very old woman, who you probably have guessed was Sunday.

*You twist the wool just so, and you spin the spindle just so.* She showed how to do those things as she wound the new thread upon the spindle.

And then you probably know the next thing that happened, which was that Ida was happy at the idea that people could make thread, because if they made thread they could weave, and if they could weave they could make cloth, and if they made cloth there could be new clothes. She thought maybe she could bring this great art to her birthday party as a gift to everyone.

Of course she wanted to try spinning, and of course Sunday was only too happy to hand her the spindle, and of course she pricked her finger on the sharp spindle and got sleepy. There was a little bed in the corner with the nicest quilt on it, fluffy as a summer cloud. She lay herself down there and shut her eyes for what she thought would be a moment.

Sunday had done what she had come to do, and she disappeared, leaving behind a spindle and the thread she had spun with it, and a door shut by locks and magic so no one could get in from below. No one else would enter the little room at the top of the tower for a hundred years.

# MAYA,
## or WAKING BEAUTY

The story you probably know tells you that she slept for a hundred years, and some princes tried to climb into the west tower to rescue her and wake her up and win her hand in marriage and thereby become the next king of Zur.

Except those weren't the rules, because nothing was going to wake her up early and she was going to wake up anyway after a hundred years, and Zur didn't do kings, just queens, lots of queens but no bosses. They were in the wrong story, and they got stuck in the thorns of the rosebushes climbing up the tower, which often happens when you're in the wrong story.

What the story of Sleeping Beauty leaves out is what happened to Maya when her older sister disappeared. Or maybe the story should have never been about the one who slept for a hundred years. Maybe it should have been about the one who stayed awake. At least this one is, which is why it's called Waking Beauty.

Maya was sad and wished she had never said any mean things to Ida and let her have the best strawberry and go first when it was time to ride the seahorse the mermaids brought. She wished, and time passed, and her parents were sad too. The people who lived all around them were sad because Ida was a much-loved child and because they knew when the old queen was gone there would be no one to sing the song that made the cherry trees bloom in the spring. It had to be the first-born girl.

But with Ida gone, people could start spinning and weaving and sewing again, and everyone got new clothes when all that was done. So when Maya turned fifteen she had a beautiful dress for her first-dance party.

By the way, she and her family lived in a corner of the palace, because when the people decided that queens shouldn't rule over them they decided that no one family needed a hundred rooms and four towers and all that. So it had become an apartment building in which many families lived. Maya and her parents had a nice apartment in one corner, and there was also a book library and a seed library and a musical library and a school and a workshop and a ballroom and a science lab and a museum and other useful things for everyone in the other parts of the old palace and the villages beyond. Both of her parents were librarians. Some of the other librarians, teachers, and nurses also lived in the palace.

The dance for her birthday was in the ballroom that everyone's dance parties were in and it was very nice. Her dress was silver with drawings of birds and blossoms she drew herself, and embroidered with the help of Tuesday, the good fairy who liked to drop by and visit sometimes, and she danced and danced and talked and talked and had a good time.

So did everyone else there, though her parents were sad as they thought of the party Ida never had and of the daughter who was sleeping sleeping sleeping in the west tower, not far away and heartbreakingly far, too far away for anyone to reach for another ninety-seven years.

～∂～

When she got older, Maya sometimes had trouble sleeping. When she did, she would saddle a horse and go ride down at night and listen to the mermaids sing where the Amandla River flowed into the Indigo Sea. She would bring paper and ink with her and draw the mermaids and the waves and the way the moonlight fell on the waves and the seabirds flew at night, pale against the dark sky.

When she was drawing she didn't think about anything else, not what had happened, not what was going to happen, not what she wished would happen. And she found that by drawing she could make things happen, if only on paper. She drew a grown-up Ida singing, she drew the cherries on the cherry trees the way they were before Ida disappeared, she drew the path to the west tower no one could find, she drew the rosebushes growing up that tower with all their roses and all their thorns. She got better and better at drawing. The old men swore that the birds she drew would fly up off the paper into the sky.

～∂～

While Maya was growing up, Ida was sleeping, and she did not get hungry or grow older. She stayed exactly fifteen years old, and the only thing that changed was that her hair grew longer, a foot a year. When she had been there thirty-three years her hair was thirty-five feet long. (It was already two feet long when she fell asleep.) And it kept growing.

The only other thing that changed was her dreams. She had long dreams. In her dreams, she was a unicorn who lived all alone in a lilac wood and learned all the things unicorns know. She was a bird who flew to where it was summer on wings as sharp as knives. She was her mother's mother's mother's mother spinning on a spinning wheel the story of all their lives.

She dreamed of snow in the winter and flowers in the summer and sometimes butterflies or snowflakes came through the open window in the little room at the top of the tower. But under the cloudy quilt she was never too warm and never too cold. In dreams she learned the language of the birds. In dreams the River Amandla was a beautiful woman who came and taught her all the songs that water sings, the roar of a waterfall and the shout of a flood, the gentle song of spring rain, the happy burble of a little stream flowing over rocks, the drumbeat of the waves on the rocks as steady as day and night, the sad song of one teardrop running down one cheek. Sometimes she didn't dream for years at a time. But she slept. And slept. And slept.

Maya became a great artist, and she became a great artist by drawing and looking at pictures and drawing and painting some more, and studying with older artists and asking herself questions, day after day, year after year. Where does the light fall? What does the ink do? How does the raindrop shine? When does the leaf curl?

When she was forty, she also became a great hero.

It was during the terribly cold winter when the wolves were so hungry they came out of the high mountains and began to prowl around the palace and the homes beyond it looking for someone or something to eat. There were so many wolves, skinny and sharptoothed, that people were afraid to go out. It was a terrible time for people and also for wolves. The wolves have their own story, and I think that during that time Ida dreamed she was a silver wolf among the wolves howling at the icicle moon.

Maya forgot to be afraid because she had an idea. She went out on her snowshoes with an ink bottle strapped to her waist and no weapon but a paintbrush as long as a sword. She let the wolves see her and the gray wolves ran after her across the snow like letters running across a sheet of white paper.

She ran lightly over the snow to the great whitewashed wall at the edge of the village. When she got there, she dipped her paintbrush in the ink that had not frozen because it was so close to her warm body. With it she painted a doorway.

She had been painting and drawing a long time and she had become really good at it, and when you get really really good at something it's pretty much the same as magic. (Everyone thinks magic just happens, but a lot of times you have to work at it. When you've worked at it a long time, it looks easy, and then people say, *Magic!*)

She leapt lightly through the doorway she had painted and the wolves followed her, but she was faster than them on the soft snow, and inside the doorway she painted a great table full of food. The hungry wolves fell on the food and thought no more of the woman they had followed. Then she painted new mountains and rivers far beyond the table. The wolves are still inside her drawing, still happy, still feasting from the table whose food never runs out.

And then Maya turned around and painted a little door that only she could slip through, painted it closed, painted a little lock shaped like a heart on it, and came back into the village, the village with no wolves. Seven people had seen her lead the wolves through the door she painted and come back alone and they told everyone else, and there was a great feast—not with painted food, but with the food people had put away for winter. The story of the artist and the wolves became a song people sang by the firesides of their homes in winter.

Many years later when they sang the story of Maya who drew the wolves away, some people would ask *Was she beautiful?*

The people who knew her best would say, *She was beautiful but she was better than beautiful. When she showed up, beauty showed up with her, all over.*

They would say, *She showed us how dew on grass in the morning or a fallen feather or the twig with two leaves was more beautiful than we had ever realized. She made us pay attention and find out how much beauty there was in in a tired horse and a toad's golden eye and the smoke when you blow a candle out. She made seeing beautiful and she taught us to see. She didn't keep all the beauty to herself. She found it everywhere and gave it to everyone.*

The days became years and the years rolled on and the spring came and the summer and then the leaves fell and the snow returned. The peach and plum trees flowered in the spring and bore fruit in the summer and lost their leaves in the fall. In the winter, snow fell very softly and piled high on every branch and twig, and then it happened all over again. The cherry trees had green leaves in the spring and lost their leaves in the fall and held their bare branches up against the winter sky, but there were no flowers and no fruit, and cherry jam and cherry pie and cherry wine were just stories that old people talked about and young people didn't really believe.

A hundred years passed, a hundred springs, a hundred falls, with the lives of others beginning and ending, and every life was another story, and Maya's two children had children, and then their children had some children too, and she lived on and painted on. Each of the children was another story, or a thousand more stories, and there were as many stories in the Land of Zur as there were gleaming drops on the grass after rain.

# ATLAS,

## or A LAD AT LAST

Once upon a time, in the land of Zakistan on the other side of the mountains from Zur, there was a boy named Atlas with big dreams and no shoes. There were no cherry trees in Zakistan, but the orchard of the golden apples of the sun at the top of the highest hill in the center of Zakistan was famous. Atlas was supposed to guard it at night. He was the youngest of three sons. Their mother was poor because she wasn't paid enough for her work fixing clocks, and their father had gone far away to look for work and not come back, so each of the boys had to go to work when they were very small.

The oldest son got a job watching over the silver deer in the great gardens of the moon. The second son got a job feeding the black swans in the Pearl River that ran through the city. And Atlas guarded the golden apples, but every night a firebird came down at night and took one. Every morning Atlas got yelled at because another golden apple was gone.

So he climbed up in the topmost tree on the hilltop night after night and tried to stop the bird from grabbing an apple, and night after night the bird grabbed an apple anyway.

One starry night, he grabbed the bird's ankles as it grabbed an apple, but the great powerful firebird with its wings full of feathers as bright as flames flew off with him. The boy was scared to be up in the air. The bird was scared to have a boy hanging onto him, and so they went across the starry sky, two frightened beings stuck together by fear and surrounded by air. The bird flew higher and higher. That night, it flew across the mountains and when the sun rose as bright as the firebird's feathers, it landed on the roof of a tower, exhausted. The boy let go of the bird. The bird let go of the golden apple, which rolled into the gutter of the tower.

Atlas grabbed the apple that shone like a little sun and put it in his pocket. He looked at the firebird, which had a face as fierce as an eagle and wings as wide as a house. The bird looked back at him with its eyes like twin fires. And then the bird flexed those mighty wings and lifted off and Atlas was alone on the pointed roof of a tower far from everything and everyone he knew. From the rooftop, he could see a river flowing down to the sea and some villages, forests, and the other three towers of the palace he had landed on top of. Behind him were the mountains he had flown over.

He was a practical boy and he knew his first task was to get off the roof. He looked around and carefully swung himself down from the gutter to a windowsill. The window was open. He jumped down from the windowsill into a round tower room.

On the far side of that room was a little bed with a quilt as soft as a summer cloud, and under the quilt a girl was sleeping. He jumped down with a thump as she opened her eyes and yawned. It was exactly a hundred years since that girl had lain down after she had pricked her finger with a spindle. Atlas didn't know that, but he did see that the hair pouring off her head was very long.

*Good morning*, he said!

*Oh hello*, she said!

*Excuse me*, he said! *I didn't know anyone was here!*

*Hello*, she said again, trying out talking after a hundred years of not seeing or speaking to another living being. It felt good to talk. And to have someone to talk to. But she also hadn't listened to anyone for a hundred years, so she was out of practice.

And then she said, *I am the sleeping beauty and you must be the prince who came to rescue me. Thank you for climbing the tower to rescue me!* (Of course she didn't need rescue or waking up; she just had to sleep for those hundred years.)

*No*, said Atlas, *I was dropped off on the roof here by the firebird! Who are you?*

*I am Sleeping Beauty and we are in the fairy tale* Sleeping Beauty, she replied.

*No*, said Atlas, *we are in the fairytale called* The Firebird *and I am the boy who flew all night hanging onto the legs of the firebird as it crossed the mountains and brought me here.*

*Sleeping Beauty!*

*Firebird!*

*You're in my story!*

*No, you're in my story!*

*I'm not a prince, for one thing*, said Atlas! *I'm a poor boy from Zakistan, and my name is Atlas.*

*See*, said Ida, *even your name is At Last.*

*No*, he said, *ATLAS!*

*At Last is such a beautiful name and it makes so much sense in my story!* said Ida.

*Atlas*, Atlas said. He shrugged.

And they began to argue, until Atlas, who was a practical boy, said,

*It doesn't matter whose story this is, but maybe we would both like to find an exit?*

They went down the staircase together, but after seventeen twists in the spiral staircase they came to an iron door that was locked. Extremely locked. Locked shut. Impassable. Not going to budge, though the two tried. It was an enchanted door, put there by Sunday.

They walked back up past the river of hair that had poured down the staircase for a hundred years and looked out the windows. A river of hair that poured from Ida's head.

*If only we had a ladder*, Ida said.

*If only we had a rope*, Atlas said.

*If only*, Ida began to say, and then she said, *I grew a rope while I was asleep. Look at my hair.* It trailed behind her as though her sister had painted a great long line in ink.

Sunday, the fairy who was so good she was terrible, had left the spindle and some scissors behind. The two young people cut her hair until it was once again just about as long as it was when she went up those stairs a hundred years ago. Then they each began to braid and they braided her hundred feet of hair into a ladder even longer than that. They rescued themselves. They pushed the little bed over to the window and hooked the ladder over it and dropped it down where it fell over the rosebushes down to the ground, and one of them went first and one of them went second and no one remembers which was which.

When they reached the ground, Atlas said, *Where are we?*

And Ida said, *Home!*

⤴

To Ida, some things looked different. But enough things looked the same that she was able to walk around the outside of the palace to the main entrance and through the gates past the library to the staircase to her family's apartment. The front door used to be painted green but when she arrived, the door was painted orange. She knocked. Someone answered who looked perfectly familiar and totally strange. She didn't know it but it was her sister's granddaughter's oldest child, Noa.

*Hello?* said Noa.

*I'm Ida*, said Ida.

*Oh my doves and dragons!* said Noa. *Come in. I have heard about you all my life!*

Maya was then a hundred and twelve years old, still painting, still thinking, still loving, still caring. But she was as old and frail as the last leaf on the tree that the cold wind is tugging at when winter is coming.

Noa told their mother that Ida was back, and soon everyone knew.

Maya was thrilled, but it took a little while to explain to Ida that a hundred years had passed and a few people had changed, and some of them were gone, and this old woman with so many descendants who had filled the home with paintings was her little sister who was twelve when Ida fell asleep.

The two sisters were reunited, and the songs say that they cried so many tears that they flowed in a stream all the way to the Amandla river, and the salty stream still flows, with golden wishing fish and tiny sea dragons swimming in it. I don't believe that myself, partly because Maya always had a handkerchief in her pocket or a rag for wiping paint. They cried, and they talked.

*Hello, younger sister*, said Ida, who was fifteen, to Maya.

*Hello, older sister*, said Maya, who was a hundred and twelve.

*Perhaps you're the older sister now?* said Ida.

*Perhaps I am, or perhaps I'm not*, said Maya, and giggled. Ida began to laugh.

*Hello, older younger sister*, said Ida, and began to laugh through her tears.

*Hello, younger older sister*, said Maya.

And Ida said, *This is At Last.*

*Atlas*, murmured Atlas, hopelessly.

Ida continued, *He helped me get out of the tower when I woke up this morning.*

Maya said to the boy, *In this land we welcome strangers from afar, and you are doubly welcome for helping my sister.*

⤳

Atlas met the family and they thanked him and offered him some porridge and a cup of tea. He was so hungry. Magic is tiring, and flying all night by clinging to the ankles of the firebird is also very tiring and very cold, and a lot had happened since his last meal. Which wasn't very big, because he was poor and often hungry.

It turned out that Ida was even hungrier, since she hadn't eaten in a hundred years. There are 365 days in a year, so Ida had missed about 36,500 breakfasts. If you laid all her missing breakfasts in a row, they would reach all the way from the palace gate to the ocean.

*You are very welcome to stay*, said Maya to Atlas. *As long as you like.*

She had a bright smile that made him smile too. But she was so frail, and she trembled like a leaf. He ate another bite of porridge. Then he remembered that he had a golden apple in his pocket. He pulled the apple out and asked her to eat it, happy that he had something to give as he was being given porridge and thanks and warmth and soup and clean socks and invitations to stay as long as he liked, even if that meant forever.

Maya took a bite of the apple and stopped trembling. She took another bite and sat up a little taller in her chair. Another and she stood up and looked stronger than she had in twenty years. Another: her eyes grew bright. Another and she looked ready to dance over to where Ida was meeting her great-nieces and nephews. Golden apples do that.

That morning the firebird landed in the window and said, because it was a talking bird, *Hey, I was going to bring her one when you grabbed me, boy. Did you think I was just a thief? I bring the apples to those who need them.*

Firebirds only talk to non-firebirds when they have something important to say. Maybe what the firebird on the windowsill of Maya's home said wasn't important, but firebirds are like everyone else when they feel that someone has blamed them for something they didn't do. Of course I was going to say that the golden-apple-delivering firebird has a story, and that's another story.

And the boy, Atlas, said, *She got it anyway.*

The bird shone. Sparks flew off its wings. A knock came at the door.

*Oh,* said the firebird, *here come the fairies.*

⁓

Tuesday and Thursday had arrived.
*What's the story, Morning Glory?*
said Thursday, and Ida, Maya, and Atlas all began to talk at once.

Oh Thursday I am so glad to see you, said Ida, and it seems that I have been asleep for a hundred years and I just got back with the help of my friend At Last and I had such strange dreams and you were in some of them and so were mermaids, rivers, stars, and secrets. I just got back and my sister is 112 years old and my parents are gone and I don't know what I'm going to do next. What happens next in the story of Sleeping Beauty? And am I the younger sister now?

I am just a poor boy who was guarding the golden apples in Zakistan and the Firebird brought me here, said Atlas, and I don't know what is going to happen to me or how to get home and I'm scared even though these are very nice people and I miss my mother already and how does the story of the Firebird end, and will I get in trouble about the apple and missing work? Thank you for asking!

Dearest Thursday, darling Tuesday, how lovely to see you, can we offer you some tea? Ida has just woken up after a hundred years, as you and your sisters promised, and thank you for what you did then, before I was born. It is so exciting to see her back. Now we know how this bit of the story ends, and some new stories begin today! I am so glad Ida is back. A hundred years is a long time to miss your sister! But about that tea!

Thursday said, *The center of the universe is everywhere, and of course it always seems to be right where you are, so there are more centers than there are drops of rain in a rainstorm or stars in the sky when the rainclouds blow away or grains of sand under the sea. I hear all your stories, and I would definitely like a cup of tea. So would Tuesday, I bet. We have heard approximately seventeen million stories apiece in our long lives, and they make us thirsty. Stories that would break your heart or set your mind on fire or make you wonder or see something for the first time or let go of something you thought mattered. You three have good stories. Noa is going to have a great story one of these days.*

Noa brought tea.

⤲

The ladder of Ida's hair can be seen in the museum today, between Maya's painting of the wolves feasting from their table of plenty and a shining feather from the firebird that was stuck in Atlas's hoodie when he first climbed off the roof of the west tower. Some people say your hair holds your memories, so perhaps that ladder holds a hundred years of dreams.

Ida was still fifteen and she had her fifteenth birthday party a hundred years late. By that time it was spring, so she sang the song that made the cherry blossoms bloom, and there was cherry pie that summer and every summer after. That's how the great cherry blossom festivals of Zur began.

She and Maya spent a lot of time together. Maya told her what had happened during the hundred years she slept. And Ida told her about her hundred years of dreams. Some of her dreams she turned into songs that are still sung today in the land of Zur. Some of her dreams Maya painted.

Atlas became a gardener and teacher, and moved into the palace. Maya's family helped him send for his mother and brothers, who came over the mountains to live with him. He became friends with Maya and Ida. And Ida learned that his name was not actually At Last. Maybe this story should be called Twelve Times Upon a Time, because Atlas also matters.

And they all lived
happily,
sadly,
busily,
quietly,
noisily,
dreamily,
sleepily,
wakefully
ever after,
or at least for a good long while,
tangled up in everyone else's story,
like all of us.

Sometimes the fairies visited, except for Sunday, who was sulking that Ida's story had ended up pretty okay.

Children in the land of Zur ask the story-
tellers

> Tell us the story of the cherry pies!
> Which is the story of Sleeping Beauty
> Which is the story of Waking Beauty
> Which is the story of Atlas and the
Firebird.

Three stories or maybe four
braided together like Ida's hair when
she and Atlas made the ladder. With
so many other stories all around them.

What's your story, Morning Glory?
How many other stories are all around
you?

# SLEEPING, WAKING, REVISING

Fairytales are rambling old structures full of wonders and troubles. The latter include both the troubles the protagonists face, since fairytales are almost always tales of overcoming difficulty and obstacles, and the troubles we have with fairytales whose worldviews no longer fit our own. I imagine them as akin to ancient houses, places we might still want to spend time in, but the roof leaks, or the pipes are lead, or maybe some bad gaslighting was installed back when people thought about these things differently. Maybe some fairytales should be razed to the ground, though I believe even Hans Christian Andersen's punitive "Little Mermaid" is capable of being salvaged and might try my hand at it one day.

But most of them should just be renovated, keeping the beautiful old handiwork—the vividness, the resolute protagonists, the enchantments and disenchantments, the emblems and metaphors—and shedding the old prejudices and outdated perspectives. The world has changed a lot in recent decades, and carrying fairytales forward so that they remain pleasurable and useful requires this revision.

Most fairytales with female protagonists reflected a world in which women's economic future depended upon finding and keeping a husband, which is not how the world works nowadays for most of us, and even when it does, it often works badly, and it's not a good moral in this era. Many fairytales are also full of social climbing, of gaining riches and status, often via spouses, and there are a lot of swineherds marrying princesses and goosegirls ending up with kings, and that definitely goes on the scrap pile for my renovations.

My Cinderella doesn't marry the prince, who also needs liberating from his confining role; it comes up with different solutions for Cinderella's bereft and exploited state. My Sleeping Beauty and her sister are daughters of a queen, but one who only holds a ritual position in a democratic society with a variety of queens (possibly some of them drag queens and definitely one of them the queen of camping, because plotting in a few jokes for adults is something I learned from the great cartoon show *The Adventures of Rocky and Bullwinkle*, when I was a kid myself). The book is divided into thirds, with the usual subject of the original "Sleeping Beauty," the firstborn daughter, featured in the first, her younger sister, the wak-

ing beauty of the title, at the center of the second third, and the last given over to a boy protagonist and a transmogrification of the wonderful Russian fairytale "The Firebird."

So there are things about fairytales that feel outdated. But also things that feel absolutely contemporary or even forward-looking. We live in a world where science gives us news that might as well be magic, about the poetic relationships between species or the migratory habits of terns and monarch butterflies or the ways starfish regenerate their limbs or just the underlying order and pattern of the world. And where some of those things are also curses, the curse of climate change and the sixth great extinction, the ways human misconduct is breaking up those patterns—or perhaps it is that we have made monsters we call corporations, behemoths and leviathans granted legal immunity and semi-immortality that seek their own interests in conflict with those of living beings. Perhaps someday they will seem as strange as dragons or goblins.

Amitav Ghosh writes, in his book on climate change and the novel, *The Great Derangement*, "Yet now our gaze seems to be turning again; the uncanny and improbable events that are beating at our doors seem to have stirred a sense of recognition, an awareness that human beings were never alone, that we have always been surrounded by beings of all sorts who share elements of that which we had thought to be most distinctively our own . . ." And he writes about how before the novel, the stories we fed on were full of the exceptional, the improbable, the enchanting. Then came the novel's bourgeois realism fixated on the probable and the everyday, with a version of everyday that often excludes wonder and the nonhuman, the natural as well as the supernatural.

We need these wilder stories in this wild time. So fairytales are very old and also very contemporary equipment for children and everyone else to face the world they will live in. (It is an unfortunate recent idea that fairytales are only for children, or that fairytale means something unbelievable, since people in other times knew very well what was true about fairytales.) In the first month of the US Covid pandemic, I began to tell fairytales live online as a way to reach out to people who felt stranded and isolated and sometimes frightened. I had the sense that particularly for children, the restrictive new order of things might seem arbitrary as well as harsh, and fairytales feature people contending with exactly those circumstances. I began one afternoon's stories with "Just because you don't know how you're going to get through something doesn't mean you aren't going to get through it. And just because you do think you know how, doesn't mean that you will get through it the way you intend."

*Waking Beauty* is a sequel to *Cinderella Liberator*, and both were prompted in part by the possibility of using the silhouette illustrations by the great children's illustrator Arthur Rackham. Those images seemed to me to suit the present, in that they might not exclude nonwhite readers as directly as his very Eurocentric color illustrations do, and they remain exquisitely beautiful and, well, enchanting. They were, unfortunately, originally paired with a particularly noxious, class-bound retellings of "Cinderella" and "Sleeping Beauty," so my goal was to keep the pictures and leave the problems behind. Besides, since *Cinderella Liberator* was dedicated to my great-niece Ella, I owed her younger sister, Maya, a book of her own, and this is it, though she has to share it with my godson Atlas.

I borrowed Atlas's and Maya's names for two of the protagonists and wove in some other family names, and enjoyed making Amanda into Amandla, a Xhosa and Zulu word for power that crowds chanted in a call-and-response with the just-freed Nelson Mandela in 1990 (and at other times in the anti-Apartheid movement in South Africa). Lots of other bits and pieces of various cultures came readily to hand. The dance for a girl's fifteenth birthday is a Latina quinceañera. The artist disappearing into her work comes from a tale about the Tang dynasty artist Wu Daozi and from Lafcadio Hearn's *The Boy Who Painted Cats* set in Japan (and a scene in the Coyote and Road Runner cartoon that fascinated me when I was a child). Cherry blossom festivals are obviously Japanese, and I borrowed the healing aspects of the golden apples from C.S. Lewis's *The Magician's Nephew*. Atlas, the protagonist in the Firebird section, owes a lot to Aladdin and other poor and resourceful characters in some of what in English is known as *The Thousand and One Nights* or *Arabian Nights* tales. Many years ago the Guatemala-born architect Teddy Cruz recruited me for a project, never realized, to turn a mansion into a multifamily dwelling, at least on paper; it was a pleasure to do so, at least on paper here with the usual palace or castle of a fairytale.

With both retellings, I tried to do a thoughtful renovation or winnowing, a careful look at what remained delightful and what no longer worked and what questions arose—like, what happens when you sleep for a hundred years and how does the world go on while you sleep? What kind of dreams do you have? Then there's the question of what we want fairytales to do. Perhaps to liberate the protagonists—who are usually young, poor, marginal, or otherwise relatively powerless—from their troubles or rather give them a chance to liberate themselves, turn their lives inside-out, and land where they should be, amid love and bounty and security. I realized that the relationship between the fairy godmother and Cinderella was more interesting and creative than that between Cinderella and the prince, and that if I wanted to liberate the girl from marrying the boy, I wanted to liberate the boy from being a prince. With "Sleeping Beauty," I had to liberate the story from centering on a girl who first suffers a curse and then sleeps for a century, which makes her a not very active protagonist, though I also tried to give her an active dream life.

I was inspired by the wonderful tradition of shifting the center of the story to another protagonist, which has often (but not always) been a feminist exercise. C.S. Lewis did it with his novel *Till We Have Faces*, recentering the ur-fairytale of Cupid and Psyche on Psyche's older sister, and Jane Smiley took the eldest daughter of Lear as her protagonist in her retelling of Shakespeare's tragedy *A Thousand Acres*. Jean Rhys wrote her scathing revision of *Jane Eyre* with the Caribbean first wife of Mr. Rochester—the despised madwoman in the attic in Charlotte Brontë's novel—at the novel's center; Pat Barker, Christa Wolf, Madeline Miller, and other women writers have retold the Greek myths and epics from the perspective of female characters recently. Of course Angela Carter had her way with the classic fairytales, and so have many others.

In this spirit, *Waking Beauty* portrays a world in which each of us is at the center of our own story and all of us exist in a forest of others' stories. Becoming aware of that is part of developing social awareness and empathy (which some kids have instinctively and some adults lack alarmingly or have been taught to sabotage). Thus the story's center shifts from Ida to Maya to Atlas, with indications of all the other life stories, from mice to fairies, that exist all around them, and ends by asking readers what their story is.

**REBECCA SOLNIT** is the author of more than twenty books including the best-selling *Men Explain Things to Me*, along with *Call Them by Their True Names*, *Hope in the Dark*, and *The Mother of All Questions*.

**ARTHUR RACKHAM** (1867–1939) was a prominent British illustrator of many classic children's books from *The Fairy Tales of the Brothers Grimm* to *Sleeping Beauty*. His watercolor silhouettes were featured in the original edition of *Cinderella*.

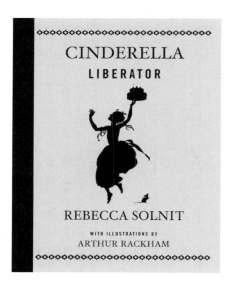

Also by Rebecca Solnit,
illustrated by Arthur Rackham